Bharatiya Katha Vaibhava - 1

(Stories for Children)

Shreedarshan K.

ZORBA BOOKS

Publishing Services by Zorba Books, October 2020
Cover Design @ Dhiraj

Zorba Books Pvt Ltd.(opc)
Sushant Arcade
Sushant Lok 1
Gurgaon 122002
India
Website: www.zorbabooks.com
Email: info@zorbabooks.com
Contact: 0124-4259579/8800509579

Print Book ISBN: 978-93-90011-66-7
Ebook ISBN: 978-93-90011-67-4

Zorba Books Pvt. Ltd.(opc)

I dedicate this book to my guru Swami Chinmayananda
of Chinmaya Mission.

I would also like to express my gratitude to members
of ''Naadopaasana Trust'' for their support and
encouragement in bringing out this book.

Preface

Stories form an integral part of our lives. Bharat is a land filled with stories which can inspire and motivate even those who have lost all hope and are in despair. Every lane in this land sings a song of a great achiever. Every monument echoes the valour of our heroes, every manuscript written by realized masters provide a direction for spiritual seekers. These immortal stories from our Epics, Puranas and History have been rewritten for our children, so they can understand, know and enjoy them. These stories provide ample evidence for us to feel proud of our rishis, saints, kings and patrons of our National and Cultural heritage.

This book is a small, humble effort to put forth such wonderful stories in front of all our young minds. I hope the young and old alike will enjoy reading them and would be inspired to follow the footsteps of their glorious ancestors.

Content

1. Sarvam Krishnamayam

The people of Vrindavan were rejoicing with Lord Krishna amidst them. The Lord's adventures and playful sports, mischief and pranks, and his love and affection were the only topics of discussion in every house. Not only the people but even the trees and animals, the cows and calves all were in blissful ecstasy. Suddenly, a strange desire arose in their minds. Every gopi wanted to experience the joy of having Krishna as her child! Every cow wanted Krishna as its calf! The trees wanted Krishna alone, to climb them! The Yamuna wanted only Krishna to play in her waters! The Lord decided to fulfil their desires.

At the same time, Lord Brahma, overwhelmed by the Lord's maya, unable to understand the true glory of the Lord, decided to test Lord Krishna's divine power. He came down and put all the boys of Vrindavan, the cows and calves under the charm of sleep and took them to his loka. He wanted to see what Krishna would do. Krishna came to know what Brahma had done and immediately,

He the ONE, multiplied Himself to become the many. He became the cowherds, cows and calves! At dusk, Krishna, as ALL OF THEM, went back to their respective homes. No one knew what had happened because everything looked normal. This went on for an entire year.

All the people, especially the gopis, were very happy. Suddenly, their children were very bright, good and obedient! The milk that the cows   gave increased in quantity, and it was divinely sweet! The calves were more endearing! It was all Krishna and Krishna ALONE in so many different forms. The whole of Vrindavan was 'Sarvam Krishnamayam'!   It was Madhuram! Madhuram! Madhuram! Everyone's desire was fulfilled!

Almost at the end of the year, Brahma came down to check on the situation in Vrindavan. To his surprise, he found everything to be absolutely normal. All the cowherds, cows and calves were in Vrindavan just as they had always been. How could all of them be in two places at the same time!?

Suddenly, in the place of each cowherd, he saw Lord Narayana Himself in all His pristine glory. Overwhelmed by the vision of so many forms of Sri Narayana, Brahma offered his salutations to the Supreme Lord. The Lord then withdrew His cosmic form. Brahma got up and discovered the charming Divine cowherd, Balagopala, in front of him. He realized the Lord's might and power; His infinite glory. He approached Lord Krishna, prostrated to Him, and prayerfully sought His forgiveness for doubting the glory of the Lord. The Lord of Compassion forgave him. All the cowherds, cows and calves he had carried to his loka returned home. They

were totally unaware of what had happened.
It was as if they had just woken up from a
deep sleep.

Brahma went back to His world reflecting on
how blessed the gopas and gopis were, how
blessed the cows and calves were, how
blessed the inhabitants of Vraja were, how
blessed the soil of Vrindavan was to carry
the tiny imprints of the lotus feet of the
Lord on its surface, and how blessed indeed
was one who was born in Vrindavan!

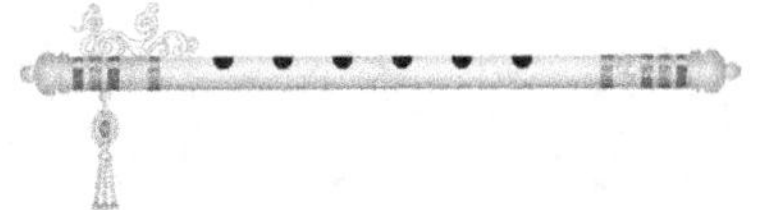

2. Story of Arjuna – The Power of Mantra

Dronacharya was the teacher of both the Pandavas and the Kauravas. Arjuna was indeed the best among all and hence, very dear to his Guru Drona. During a class, Dronacharya was telling them about the power of mantras. He told them that when one invokes Lord Varuna (God of water) and releases an arrow, it becomes Varunastra which brings rain. Similarly, when Lord Agni (God of fire) is invoked by chanting the relevant mantra, the arrow becomes Agni-astra.

Since these mantras were taught to all the students, Arjuna was doubtful whether their concentration was good enough to invoke the powers of the mantra when chanted. In order to remove his student's doubts and test their abilities, Dronacharya decided to test them. He asked all his students to take some sealed pots and fill them with water. Each pot only had a small hole – the size of a pepper. The winner would be the one who managed to fill a pot with water first.

All of them took the sealed pots and went to a nearby lake to fill them with water. Despite keeping the pot immersed for long, water hardly entered the pot. Arjuna's pot too remained almost empty. He then realized that his Guru had taught him the mantra to invoke Lord Varuna. If he invoked Lord Varuna, the pot would get filled automatically. Arjuna chanted the relevant mantra in order to fill the pot. Soon, the pot filled up with water.

All the other Pandavas and Kauravas returned disappointed. When Dronacharya asked Arjuna for his pot, he went up to his teacher with the water filled pot. He told his Guru that he had invoked Lord Varuna to fill the pot. Dronacharya was pleased and told the other students to be disciplined and put in effort like Arjuna.

3. The Power of 'Rama Naama'

The vanaras had assembled at the southern tip of Bharat, all eager to cross the ocean and fight the wicked demon, Ravana. Between them and Lanka stood the mighty ocean. A mighty bridge was being built with the help of huge rocks to cross the ocean. All the rocks had been brought to Hanuman, and 'Sri Rama' was written on each rock. The huge rocks were given to 'Nala' who was the commander-in-chief of the vanaras. He, along with his brother Nila, was responsible for building the entire bridge across the ocean.

As he watched the rocks floating on water with astonishment, just by the power of His name, Lord Rama himself decided to throw a small pebble in the water to check if it would float. Rama took a small pebble and dropped it in the ocean and it sank, which always happens when a pebble is dropped in water. The Lord wondered why a small pebble sank when He Himself had dropped it, whereas the huge rocks that had 'Sri Rama' written on them floated.

Hanuman had watched all the happenings and at once came to the Lord, and said that whatever happened was bound to happen! Anything released or dropped from the Lord's hands would sink; whether it was an inert stone or a living being—if the Lord leaves us, we are sure to sink! The Lord's hand is always there, holding us and saving us from all problems and difficulties. Even if we leave Him, HE LEAVES US NOT!!

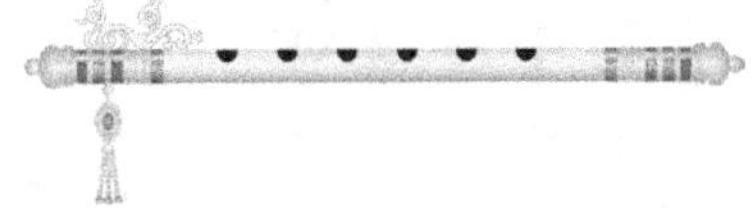

4. Merit of Feeding the Poor – Story of Sant Eknath

Eknath was a great devotee of Lord Krishna. He is said to have been born in the year 1533 CE in Maharashtra.

One day, Eknath had to perform funeral rites for his ancestors. According to the prevailing tradition, whoever was performing the rites was expected to feed the brahmanas. Instead, Eknath had invited the poor and low-caste people to his house to feed them. He served all of them with great respect.

The brahmanas got to know about this and were furious. They went to Eknath's house and accused him of having gone against the tradition of feeding the brahmanas, a grave sin. They instructed Eknath to take a bath in the river to repent for his wrong deed, and pray to God to pardon him. Without saying a single word, Eknath did what he was told.

When Eknath had just finished taking a bath in the river, a leper came there searching for Eknath. He fell at Eknath's feet and pleaded Eknath to protect him. He said that he was a devotee of Lord Shiva and had come from Tryambakeshwar. Lord Shiva had come in his dream and told him that Eknath had accumulated a lot of merit (punya) by feeding poor and low-caste people, and would be able to cure him.

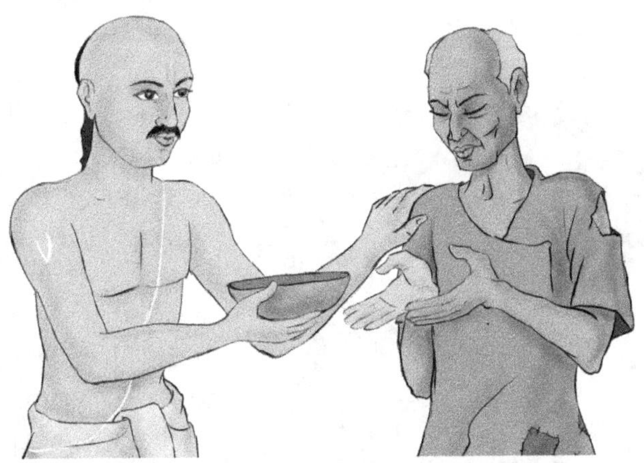

When he heard this, Eknath immediately took a handful of water from the river and sprinkled it on the leper. What a miracle! The leper was completely cured. The brahmanas who witnessed the miracle realized Eknath's greatness and pleaded for forgiveness.

Eknath later wrote a version of the Bhagavata Purana, known as Eknathi Bhagavatha, and a version of the Ramayana, known as Bhavarth Ramayana.

Moral - Jana seva is Janardana seva: 'Service to people is Service to God'.

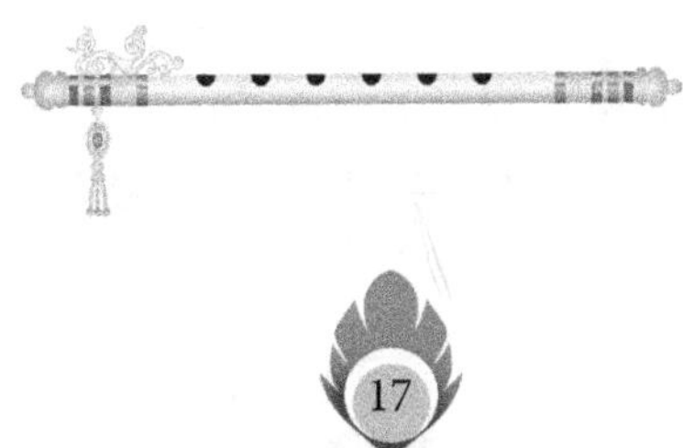

5. Shivaji Maharaj Blessed by Lord Vitthala

On the day of Ekadashi, Sant Tukaram arrived at Vithoba temple in Pune. The devotees at the temple were glad that they could hear bhajans sung by Sant Tukaram. Shivaji Maharaj unexpectedly went to the temple to hear the bhajans when he was told that Sant Tukaram was there. Shivaji Maharaj considered Sant Tukaram as his guru just like Samartha Ramadas.

It was not safe for Shivaji to stay at the temple for very long, since the enemy king was bent on capturing him. When the enemies got to know that Shivaji was at the temple, they thought it was the right time to capture him. While the bhajans were being sung, Shivaji's bodyguard told him that it was not safe for him to stay there as the enemies had come to know of his presence at the temple.

At once, Shivaji went to Sant Tukaram to take his leave. Unaware of the situation, Sant Tukaram insisted that Shivaji take prasad after the bhajan and then leave. Tukaram said that Lord Vittala would take care of everything. Shivaji decided that he would not disobey his Guru's words. He submitted himself completely at Lord Vittala's feet. Tukaram was singing bhajans with great devotion when one of his disciples went to him and said that they were surrounded by enemies eagerly waiting to capture Shivaji.

Realizing the seriousness of the situation, his heart was overwhelmed with devotion and eyes filled with tears. Tukaram invoked Lord Vittala through four beautiful abhangs, asking the Lord to take care of the entire situation. It is said that at that moment, the enemies who had surrounded the temple saw Shivaji disappearing into the forest on horseback. The enemies followed Shivaji at once. It was Lord Vittala who had taken on the form of Shivaji and disappeared into the forest.

Meanwhile, the real Shivaji escaped after taking prasad and Tukaram's blessings. Tukaram who came to know about the situation shed tears in ecstasy thinking about Lord Vittala's compassion.

Where there is unconditional devotion and complete surrender, Lord Krishna says in the Bhagavad Gita, "I shall look after your Yoga-Kshema."

[Shivaji Maharaj, born in 1630 CE was the greatest among the Maratha kings]

6. Swaminatha: The Guru of Lord Shiva

Once, Lord Brahma went to meet Lord Shiva. When he reached Lord Shiva's abode, Mt. Kailash, he ignored and disregarded the presence of the little child, Kartikeya, Lord Shiva's son. Kartikeya was displeased with Brahma's behaviour. Immediately, he questioned Brahma about the fundamental principles based on which he was proceeding with the process of creation. Brahma said that he was following the principles enshrined in the Vedas for creation. When he heard this, Subramanya asked Brahma to recite the portions from the Vedas that described the process of creation. Lord Brahma started his recitation with the Pranava Mantra, 'OM'.

As soon as Lord Brahma uttered the word 'OM', Subramanya stopped him and asked him to explain the meaning of 'OM'. Brahma was taken by surprise. He realized that he had no answer to the child's question. A creator who was incapable of explaining the meaning of 'OM' was indeed unfit to carry on the process of creation, and had to be punished. As the commander-in-chief of the Devatas, Subramanya imprisoned Lord Brahma and took up the entire process of creation upon himself!

All the devatas went and prayed to Lord Shiva seeking Lord Brahma's release. Shiva went to Subramanya and asked his son to release Brahma, but Subramanya refused stating that the Creator did not even know the meaning of the Pranava mantra 'OM', and hence, he should not be shouldering the responsibility of the creation of the world. Lord Shiva asked his son if he knew the true essence of the Pranava mantra 'OM' to which Kartikeya replied in the affirmative. Shiva asked him to impart the knowledge of the Pranava Mantra to him. Kartikeya agreed to initiate his father into the secrets of the Pranava on one condition. First, Shiva had to accept him as his Guru, and appropriately give him a higher seat than the student. The Lord agreed to accept his son as his Guru, and give him a higher place than himself. The Lord then lifted his son in his arms. Carried by his father in his arms, Kartikeya—the Guru—whispered the entire knowledge of the Pranava Mantra into his disciple's ears. At that point, Parvati came and saw her son teaching her husband! She was pleased. The Guru (Swami) was initiating her husband (Natha). She looked at her son very lovingly and said that in the future her son, Kartikeya would be known as SWAMINATHA – 'The Guru of Lord Shiva', and the sacred place where the initiation took place would be famously known as SWAMIMALAI (Tamil Nadu).

Swamimalai is one of the six main abodes of Lord Subramanya. In Swamimalai, Lord Shiva's shrine is located in the basement and Swaminatha's shrine is located atop a hillock. Sixty steps lead to the shrine, each step representing one year of the sixty years in the Hindu calendar.

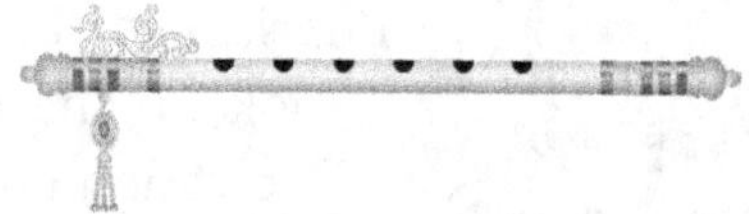

7. The Saint who Became a King – Murthi Nayanar

The Nayanars were a group of 63 saints who lived between the 6th and 8th century AD in Tamil Nadu. They were devotees of Lord Shiva. Murthi Nayanar was the 15th among the Nayanars.

Murthi Nayanar served Lord Shiva by preparing sandal paste and offering it to the Shivalinga at the Chokkanathar temple in Madurai. Then, Madurai was ruled by a Pandiyan king who was also a great devotee of Lord Shiva.

One day, the peaceful Pandiyan kingdom was attacked by a foreign Vaduka ruler who killed the Pandiyan king and ordered that no one was henceforth allowed to worship Lord Shiva. Afraid of the new king's order, people stopped going to Shiva temples, but Murthi Nayanar continued offering sandal paste to Lord Shiva. When the king came to know about it, he ordered that no one should sell sandalwood to Nayanar.

Unable to find sandalwood, Murthi Nayanar, in his devotion, thought of offering his hands that had prepared sandalwood paste all these years to the Lord. He decided to grind his hands, and his hands started bleeding. Pleased with Nayanar's devotion, Lord Shiva immediately appeared and said that the king who had disrupted Nayanar's worship would be punished for his evil deeds soon. He also said that Murthi Nayanar would rule the kingdom instead. By the Lord's grace, Murthi Nayanar's wounds were healed at once and the foreign king who had no children died a mysterious death the very next day.

As per the prevailing tradition, the ministers decided to give a garland to the royal elephant and make it walk through the streets to select the next king. The blindfolded elephant roamed the city and finally reached the temple. As soon as Murthi Nayanar came out from the temple, the elephant garlanded him.

Murthi Nayanar was taken to the palace on the royal elephant in a procession and crowned as the king. Murthi ruled in the garb of a Shaiva devotee, smearing his body with sacred ash and wearing rudraksha as ornaments and matted hair instead of a crown. He sacrificed the luxuries of the crown and ruled the kingdom justly.

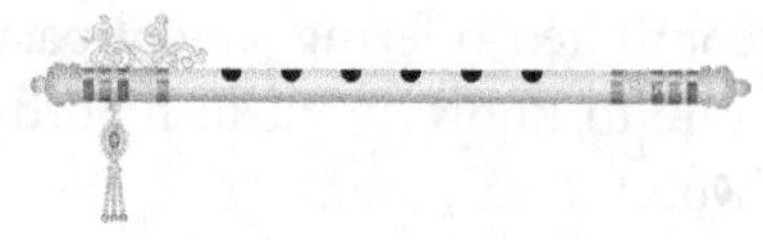

8. The Divine Grace of the Guru

Adi Sankaracharya was the greatest among the Indian philosophers. He is considered to be an incarnation of Lord Shiva. In his short life spanning 32 years, he walked the length and breadth of our country, Bharat, to bring about an awareness in the minds of the people about the principle of spiritual oneness underlying the diversity of this great subcontinent.

Sankaracharya established four mathas (monasteries) in the North, South, East, and West of India to spread Advaita philosophy. They are Sringeri in the south, Dwaraka in the west, Badri in the north and Puri in the east. Four prominent disciples of Adi Sankaracharya were the first heads of these Mathas. Totakacharya was the first head of Badri Matha.

Totakacharya was a young boy when he met Adi Sankaracharya. At that time, his name was Giri. As a student of Adi Sankara, Giri was very disciplined and hardworking, but not very bright. Every day, he would watch the beaming faces of the disciples when they grasped the teachings of the Master. Giri often felt

that he was not blessed with the intelligence to follow and understand the lessons taught by Adi Sankaracharya. However, with great faith and devotion, he continued his service to the Acharya cheerfully.

Once, Giri was washing the Master's clothes when Adi Sankaracharya sat down to begin the class. Since Giri had not yet arrived, Sankaracharya waited for him to complete his daily chores. One of the disciples politely asked the Master his reason for not starting the class. The Acharya replied that Giri had not yet come to the class. The other disciples exclaimed that it would not matter as Giri was not bright enough to understand the teachings. Adi Sankaracharya calmly replied that Giri was an attentive listener, even if he was not very bright.

At that moment, Sankaracharya decided to bless Giri for his devoted service and hard work. He mentally bestowed Giri all the knowledge of the spiritual sciences and the Vedas.

The student, who was busy with his daily chores, suddenly felt that he was completely soaked in the grace and blessings of his Guru. He collected the clothes and made his way to his Guru. He prostrated at Adi Shankaracharya's feet. In that ecstatic moment, he recited a beautiful Sanskrit poem in the totaka meter, in praise of Adi Sankaracharya. The disciples were astonished at the miraculous change and total transformation in Giri. They were surprised by the deep and profound meaning of the verses, recited by one who had not even been able to speak a single Sanskrit sentence correctly till a few moments ago. This poem came to be known as Totakashtakam. Thus, a humble student, Giri, became Totakacharya. He became one among the four prominent disciples of Adi Sankaracharya.

9. Gajendra Moksha

Gajendra, the king of the elephants, very powerful and strong, was sporting in the beautiful lush green forest lands in the valley of the Trikuta mountains, along with his herd of female companions. After a while, exhausted, they all entered into a beautiful lake to quench their thirst. Unaware of the danger awaiting them in the form of a crocodile, they started sporting in the waters.

A crocodile who lived in the lake grabbed the foot of Gajendra and started pulling him underwater. The elephant tried to release itself from the jaws of the crocodile with all its strength and might. But in vain. There ensued a great tug-of-war between the two. All the other elephants tried to help but failed to help Gajendra. Gradually, unable to rescue their king from the crocodile's jaws, they left the site. The crocodile seemed to become stronger and stronger while the lonely elephant started getting exhausted.

At that point of time, realizing its utter helplessness, the elephant sought refuge at the feet of the Lord. Gajendra plucked a lotus

from the lake, held it up in its trunk and invoked Lord Sri Hari with a beautiful, ardent prayer: 'Narayana Akhila Guro Bhagavan Namaste'. The entire invocation is known as 'Gajendra Stuti'. The Lord, known as the Saviour of the afflicted, out of infinite compassion, alighted on his vehicle, Garuda, and immediately came to Gajendra's rescue. Sri Hari released his Sudarshan chakra, which instantly killed the crocodile. The Lord Himself pulled Gajendra out of the lake and rescued him.

Spiritual Significance: Gajendra represents an individual living amidst temptations, fallen into the lake of samsara and seized by the crocodile called 'ego'. Any amount of effort to release oneself from this monstrous ego is futile. Left all alone in life's journey, the only refuge is the Lord. The moment we invoke the Lord with all our faith, devotion and knowledge (represented by the lotus), the Lord immediately comes and saves us from drowning in the pool of samsara. The ego is destroyed by the Sudarshan. When the ego is eliminated, what remains is 'Sudarshana', the 'Divine Vision', the State of Enlightenment.

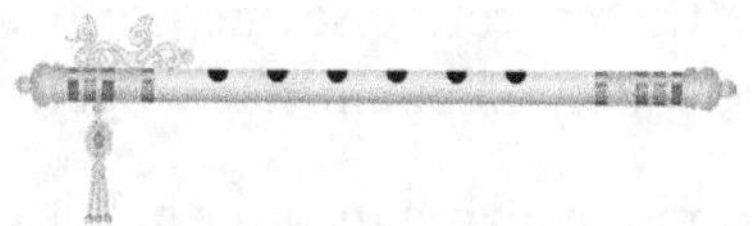

10. Devotion
-The Milkmaids of Vrindavan

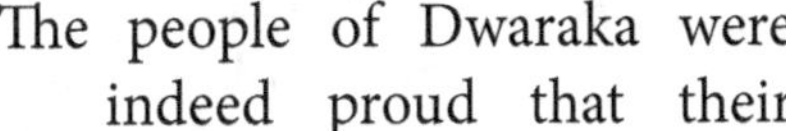

The people of Dwaraka were indeed proud that their devotion to Lord Krishna was supreme. Realizing this, Lord Krishna decided to teach them the essence of genuine devotion.

One day, the Lord collapsed on the bed crying that he had an unbearable headache. At once, the queens and Sage Narada who had come to have darshan of the Lord, immediately summoned Dhanvantri (Lord of medicine). Dhanvantri came and gave medicine to Krishna, but the Lord's headache would not go away. Since even Dhanvantri could not cure the Lord, Narada asked the Lord to suggest the cure for his pain.

Lord Krishna told Narada that the medicine to make his headache go away was the dust of the feet of a genuine devotee, which, when applied to his forehead, would cure him completely. Everyone was shocked when they heard this. Narada approached the Lord's wives to see if they would provide the dust of their feet. They refused saying that they would go to hell if the dust of their feet

was applied on the Lord's forehead. None of the people in Dwaraka obliged fearing the sin that would incur to them if they provided the dust of their feet.

Finally, Narada approached the Lord for a solution. Krishna asked Narada to go to Vrindavan and approach the gopis. Narada immediately went to Vrindavan. As soon as they saw Sage Narada, all the gopis went running up to him and offered their pranams. Narada narrated the whole incident to them. He told them that the Lord was suffering from a terrible headache, and he had come to collect the dust of the feet of a genuine devotee.

One of the gopis immediately went and brought a piece of cloth, spread it on the ground, and all the gopis stamped their feet on the cloth. They folded the cloth with the dust of their feet carefully, and asked Narada to take it and apply it to the Lord's forehead. Narada was surprised. He asked the gopis whether they were not worried of the sin they might incur, which might result in them suffering in hell. At once, the Gopis replied that they were ready to go to hell and suffer any amount of pain, if only they could relieve the Lord of his pain.

Narada returned to the Lord with the cloth filled with the dust of the gopi's feet, and narrated what had happened in Vrindavan to everyone. The Lord's headache had vanished. Krishna got up and smilingly looked at everyone assembled there. The wives of the Lord and the people of Dwaraka realized the supreme devotion of the simple, humble milkmaids of Vrindavan—the gopis.

11. Full Moon on an Amavasya Night!

Subramanya Iyer was a great devotee of Devi Abhirami (Parvathi) of Tirukadaiyur. He would sit for hours, lost in contemplation, in front of Devi. His devotion was so intense that he looked upon all women as a manifestation of Mother Goddess. He would run to them and fall flat at their feet addressing them as 'O, Mother!', whether in the temple or on the street. People even thought he was mad.

Serfoji I Bhonsle, who was the king of the Thanjavur Maratha Empire from 1712 – 1728 CE, came to the temple for darshan on a particular **new-moon day**. Everybody there made way for him. But Subramanya was sitting right in front of the deity, completely immersed in dhyana. When the king saw Subramanya thus seated in front of Devi, he enquired about him. He was told by the people around that Subramanya was an insane person. To test this, the king put forth a question to Subramanya, asking him about the **'tithi'** that day. Subramanya, who was in ecstasy, mentally seeing nothing but Devi's divine face, beautiful and shining like the full-moon in the autumn sky, blurted out that it was a **full-moon day!** The angry king walked away, threatening Subramanya that if he failed to see the full-moon at dusk, Subramanya would be burnt alive.

The temple priest woke Subramanya up from his meditation and explained what had happened. Subramanya was unperturbed. He said, "My divine Mother made me utter these words and so, it is now Her responsibility to keep up Her words."

Subramanya was made to climb onto a suspended wooden plank that was slowly being lowered. Down below was raging fire. It was dusk. Subramanya invoked His Mother, Sri Abhirami, with beautiful verses. When he had just completed the 79th verse, Goddess Abhirami gave darshan to him in the skies. She removed Her diamond ear-ornament and tossed it into space. It stood there in the sky shining like the **full-moon** for all to see! Subramanya continued to sing Her praises. The ropes snapped, the fire got extinguished by itself. The king realized his mistake and sought forgiveness from the great devotee of Sri Abhirami. Subramanya was henceforth called 'Abhirami Bhattar'. His beautiful collection of verses are known as Abhirami Anthaadi. Anthaadi means 'End – Beginning'. The last word of each verse is the beginning of the next verse! Even to this day, devotees sing these verses on Amavasya and Poornima days at Devi's altar.

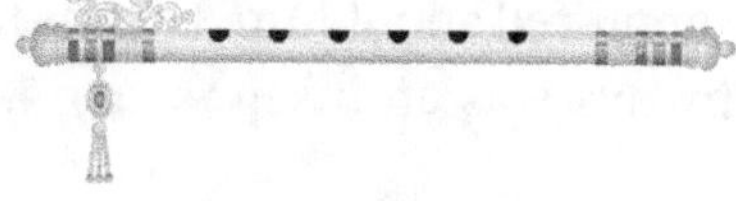

12. A Palace Becomes a Temple for Lord Rama

The Chaturbhuj temple is dedicated to Lord Vishnu. It is situated in Orchha (16 kilometres from Jhansi), in Madhya Pradesh and was built in the 16th century. The temple is known for having one of the tallest vimana standing at 344 feet! Lord Krishna and Radha are worshipped there.

The temple was constructed by the Bundela Rajputs in the 16th century, who ruled over the kingdom of Orchha at that time. The then ruler Madhukar Shah's wife, Ganeshkuwari, had a dream in which Lord Rama instructed her to build a temple for the Lord. The Queen walked all the way to Ayodhya to bring Lord Rama. On reaching Ayodhya, near the banks of the Sarayu river, she undertook a vow of fasting and prayed to Lord Rama. Unable to have darshan of the Lord, she decided to jump into the river and give up her life.

At that moment, something miraculous happened! Lord Rama appeared in the form of a child in the queen's lap. Lord Rama told the queen that he was happy with her prayers and she could ask for a boon. The queen asked Rama to come with her as a child to Orchha. The Lord agreed but put three conditions. Firstly, He would travel only on the day of Pushya nakshatra. When the nakshatra ends, he would stop and resume again when Pushya sets in. Secondly, the Lord would be the king of Orchha instead of her husband. Thirdly, since the Lord would travel in the form of a child in the queen's lap, the first place where she seated the Lord would be the final place of His stay, and the Lord would be known as Ram Raja.

The Queen agreed and started her journey back to Orchha with baby Rama in her lap. Since she could only travel during Pushya nakshatra, it took 8 months and 27 days for the queen to reach Orchha from Ayodhya on foot (between 1574 and 1575 CE). On her return to Orchha, the queen went back to her palace with baby Rama and retired to her room for the night. She planned to take Lord Rama to the Chaturbhuj temple the next day. She had forgotten the third condition that had been put forth by the Lord. The place where child Rama was placed first by the queen in the palace became his permanent abode. Hence, Lord Rama transformed into an idol and was transfixed in the queen's palace itself. To this day, the Ram Raja temple is in the queen's palace.

Lord Rama's idol continued to be worshiped in the palace and the palace was converted to the **"Ram Raja temple"**. Raja Ram is accompanied by Sita (on the left), Lakshmana, Sugreeva, and Lord Narasimha (on the right). Durga Maa, Hanuman and Jambavant are also present in the darbaar. The specialty of this temple is that Lord Rama has a sword in his right hand and a shield in the other. Shri Rama is sitting in Padmasana, with the left leg crossed over the right thigh. In India, this is the only temple where **Lord Rama is worshiped as a king** and that too in a palace. A Guard of Honour is held every day, police personnel have been designated as guards at the temple, much in the manner of a king. The food and other amenities provided to the deity at the palace-temple are similar to that offered to a king. Armed salutation is provided to Lord Rama every day.

Lord Krishna is instead worshipped in the Chaturbhuj temple that had been initially built for Lord Rama, and Lord Rama made the palace His place of worship!

13. Little Krishna and the Fruit Seller

In Vrindavan, there was a poor lady who would sell fruits in the streets. On a particular day, she could not sell a single fruit. Feeling helpless, she went to people's houses to try and sell them some fruit. Little Krishna was at home at that time. He heard the fruit-seller calling out to people to buy fruits.

Lord Krishna (the Karma Phala Dhata, the Dispenser of Fruits-of-Action to all), ran inside the house to collect some food grains in both his hands, so that he could buy fruits in exchange for the food grains. Alas! Most of the food-grains slipped through his fingers, and by the time he was at the door, his hands were almost empty. He looked at her helplessly but lovingly and gave her the few grains he still had in his hands.

The fruit-seller was so pleased with his charming innocence that she filled up both his hands with fruits, with almost nothing in exchange for it. Her basket was empty. She put the few grains

Krishna had given her into the basket and walked back home with an inexplicable smile and total satisfaction. When she reached home and put the basket down, she was in for a surprise, the whole basket was full of precious gems!

The Lord had blessed the fruit-seller immensely for her unconditional and selfless Devotion!!

14. Sri Hanuman and the Music Competition

Narada and Tumburu are well-known celestial musicians who constantly sing the glories of Lord Vishnu. Once, when Sri Hari praised Tumburu's music, Narada became very unhappy. The Lord then sent Narada to learn music from the music teacher of the celestial musicians, Ganabandhu. Still not up to the mark, he went and learnt music from Rukmini, Lord Krishna's consort. After he felt that he had had sufficient training, Narada wanted the Lord to judge Tumburu and him, and declare who was the best musician amongst the two. Narada and Tumburu sang with all their devotion unto the Lord. Both of them were very good and the Lord did not want to displease anyone by naming one of them as the winner of the competition. He thought of a simple solution, and decided to call an expert and accomplished musician for the task. He summoned Hanuman, who is Kavya - Nataka - Sangeeta - Natya - Paripoorna!!

Hanuman came and the contest started. Tumburu sang, accompanied by his veena - Kalavathi. His music was so enchanting that the whole universe of things and beings came to a standstill, almost froze and became silent! Hanuman nodded in appreciation. Next, it was Narada's turn. He rendered his music accompanied by his veena - Mahathi. Narada's music melted all that which was previously frozen! Both of them were exceptionally good. Everyone was eagerly awaiting Hanuman's judgement.

Hanuman asked for both their veenas and removed the frets of the veenas (small raised metal bars across the long thin part of a stringed musical instrument), gave their veenas back to them, and asked them to play the veena. Rather annoyed, they asked him how the veena could be played without the frets. Hanuman silently took the fretless veena and played on it using a small piece of a bamboo stick. He was an expert in playing the veena with or without frets. He continued singing and playing the fretless veena. All the devatas were lost in the divine ecstatic devotional outpouring of Hanuman. After some time, when they looked around, they found Lord Sri Hari present amongst them listening in rapt attention to Hanuman's sangeeta.

Narada and Tumburu bowed down and acknowledged that indeed Hanuman was not only the greatest devotee of the Lord, but also the most accomplished musician!!

15. Enchanting Divine Eyes that Stole the Heart!

Dhanurdas was a wealthy businessman and a good wrestler who lived in Srirangam. He got acquainted with the temple dancer, Hemamba, who was extremely beautiful. Her eyes, especially, were most captivating and Dhanurdas was lost in admiration for them! Very often, he could be seen carrying an umbrella over her head protecting her from the scorching sun.

Once, she wished to participate in the annual temple procession of Lord Sri Ranganatha, the presiding deity of Srirangam. They went to the procession together.

Sri Ramanujacharya, one of the greatest saint philosophers (born in the year 1017 AD), was also there along with his devotees to witness the beautiful procession of Lord Ranganatha. The mangala vadya was playing, the hymns were being chanted and everybody's eyes were in the direction in which the Lord's procession was about to enter the street. Sri Ramanujacharya's eyes suddenly fell on the couple. The Acharya saw the young man, Dhanurdas, gazing intensely in the opposite direction at Hemamba. Enamoured by her beauty and especially her eyes, Dhanurdas kept looking at her, continuing to cover her head with an umbrella to protect her eyes from the sun's rays! He did not even bother to turn around and look at the Lord's procession.

Seeing such a public display of enslavement to physical beauty, Sri Ramanujacharya was filled with compassion for this mortal soul. He summoned Dhanurdas and asked him what made him turn away from the Lord, when everyone present there was craving for a glimpse of the Lord. Without batting an eyelid, he said, "Her beautiful and enchanting eyes! I have not seen a pair of eyes more beautiful than these!" The Acharya challenged him and said he could show him a more beautiful pair of eyes – the most beautiful in the whole world. Dhanurdas said it was impossible. Sri Ramanujacharya insisted. Dhanurdas accepted the challenge and said if it were true, if he found the eyes more enchanting and captivating than Hemamba'a eyes, he would follow that person henceforth.

Sri Ramanujacharya asked Dhanurdas to follow him. They entered the Sri Ranganatha Swamy temple. The Acharya went inside the inner sanctum and invoked the Lord: 'O! Lord, most Compassionate One! Here is a lost soul who can be reclaimed and redeemed if you but cast one loving glance at him'. The doors were opened to have darshan of the Lord. The Lord's divine, beautiful, and captivating eyes

moved! The Lord's grace descended on Dhanurdas. Witnessing the never before seen Lord's resplendent divine form and captivating eyes, Dhanurdas broke down and surrendered himself completely to the Lord. Dhanurdas subsequently became one of the greatest disciples of Sri Ramanujacharya. He became one of the greatest Bhagavathottama, whose devotion to Lord Ranganatha was considered to be on par with that of the Azhwars.

16. Bhavaji who Played "Game of Dice" with the Lord!

Bhavaji was a saint from North India. He was a great devotee of Lord Rama. Once, he went on a pilgrimage to Tirumala (Tirupati). The quiet and serene atmosphere of the Tirumala Hills was so captivating that he decided to stay there. He made a small kutia for himself and daily visited the Lord Venkateswara temple, standing there for hours in front of the deity in whom he saw the Lord of his heart—Sri Rama. The temple priests got annoyed with his constant presence over there and told him to go away.

The next day and the day after, when he went to the temple, they refused to allow him into the temple. He pleaded for a glimpse of his Lord, but they refused to let him into the temple. With a heavy heart, he went back to his humble hut and cried his heart out to the Lord. At night, he couldn't sleep. In order to keep himself occupied, he started playing the game of dice. He played for both the parties—he on one side and the Lord on the other side! After some time, he fell asleep. While he was asleep, he had a vision. The Lord appeared in front of him and asked him to get up and play the game of dice with Him. He woke up and found the Lord in front of him. His joy knew no bounds! He and the Lord played the game of dice, and the Lord was defeated. When the Lord asked him what he wanted in return, Bhavaji's request was that every day the Lord should come and play the game of dice with him. The Lord assured him that he would do so, and as promised, the next day the Lord came to Bhavaji's place. They played the game for a while, after which the Lord rested while Bhavaji sang for Him. This went on for a few days.

One day, the Lord hurriedly left after the dice-game. The gem studded necklace that the Lord was wearing slipped down unnoticed and was left behind. When Bhavaji saw it later, he picked it up and kept it safely to return it to the Lord the next day. In the meantime, when the priests opened the temple doors in the morning, they found the necklace of the Lord missing. The temple authorities were informed. The priests who disliked Bhavaji and had denied him entry into the temple suspected him. The search party reached Bhavaji's place. They made enquires, and without a word Bhavaji immediately brought the necklace from inside. He told them that the Lord had accidentally left it behind the previous night when He had come to his dwelling to play the dice-game. Nobody believed Bhavaji. He was accused of stealing and covering it up with a fictional story.

The matter was taken to Krishnadevaraya, the king of the Vijayanagar Empire. The king saw the innocent face of the Lord's devotee and suggested a test for him instead of punishing him immediately. Bhavaji was locked up in a cell with a huge stack of sugarcane, which he had to consume and finish by the next morning. The cell was closed and guards were posted outside. Bhavaji prayed fervently to Lord Rama and was lost in contemplation. Lo! A majestic elephant appeared in the cell. Within a few minutes, it consumed the entire bulk of sugarcane and woke up Bhavaji from his meditation with a huge trumpet. He was overwhelmed to see Lord Rama, in the form of an elephant, who had come to save him. He again and again prostrated to the Lord. The guards heard the elephant's trumpet and rushed inside the cell. All the sugarcane had vanished. They had a glimpse of an elephant hurriedly leaving.

The matter was reported to the king. Everyone came rushing. They saw an overwhelmed Bhavaji looking at the site where the elephant stood and uttering the words: 'Hathi Ram! Hathi Ram!'. When the king heard about this, he and the priests asked Bhavaji for forgiveness. Later, he was made the Chief Priest of Venkateswara temple for many years. Since he was a devotee of Lord Rama, who had appeared as Hathi (elephant), he came to be known as 'Hathiram Bhavaji'. In the North, Lord Venkateswara is addressed as 'Balaji', which is attributed to him. The Hathiramji Mutt was established in his name, and it exists even to this day. The Mahants of the Mutt used to administer the Tirumala Temple from 1843 to 1932 CE till the present Tirumala Tirupati Devasthanam Board was created.

17. Sindoora Varna Hanuman

Sri Hanuman was the greatest devotee of Lord Rama. Lord Rama and Sita considered him to be their first son. Hanuman was always ready to do anything for Lord Rama, ever at His service.

Once, Hanuman saw Sita applying sindoor on her forehead. It is a tradition for all married Hindu women to apply sindoor in the parting of their hair. As he was a brahmachari, ever immersed in chanting the name of his Lord, Hanuman was unaware of the purpose of married women applying sindoor. Innocently, he asked Sita why she applied sindoor daily in the parting of her hair. She smilingly replied that applying the sindoor would increase the longevity of her Lord, Sri Rama. She did not mention the word

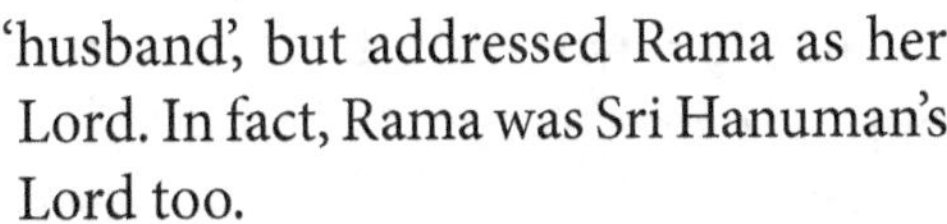

'husband', but addressed Rama as her Lord. In fact, Rama was Sri Hanuman's Lord too.

When he came to know the reason for applying sindoor, Hanuman thought to himself, would not the Lord's longevity increase even more if sindoor is applied all over the body? That would increase the life-span of Lord Rama a lot more. Sita's words went straight to his heart. He waited for Sita to leave her room and immediately went inside. He saw the little sindoor box on the table. He was not satisfied. He wanted much more, so he looked around the room. In one of the room's corners, he found a big jar full of orange powder. He quickly brought some water, poured it into the jar, stirred it, and poured the sindoor all over his body. He was dripping from head to toe with the sindoor liquid!

With the wet sindoor dripping all over, and a huge victorious smile on his face, Hanuman went to the darbar. Everyone was shocked to see Hanuman in this new avatar. Some of them were amused as well. Sri Rama was also taken aback, but knowing that Hanuman never did anything without a sound reason, he asked Hanuman to explain why he had drenched himself in the orange colour. Sita immediately understood and smiled! Hanuman narrated his conversation with Mother Sita and said that he had applied sindoor all over his body because he wished for Lord Rama a very long life! The Lord, seeing Hanuman's devotion for him, was supremely happy.

Hanuman knew that Lord Rama was the incarnation of the Supreme Parabrahma. Still, due to his unlimited love for the Lord, he decided to apply sindoor all over his body for the Lord's sake!

Since then, Hanuman has been worshiped as Sindoora Varna Hanuman. It is a tradition to offer sindoor to Sri Hanuman in temples, and this is distributed as prasad.

18. Sripadaraya: An Exemplary Guru

Sri Sripadaraya was one among the eight prominent Haridasas of Karnataka. He is considered to be the founder of the Haridasa movement in the 14th century, along with Narahari Tirtha. He was the pontiff of Madhvacharya Mutt in Mulbaagilu (a town in the Kolar District in the state of Karnataka), and is credited with the invention of the suladi (a musical rendering of devotional verses).

During his lifetime, Sripadaraya taught sarvamula granthas (Acharya Madhva's works collectively are known as Sarvamula)

forty times to forty different batches of students. He was an exemplary guru, and would give personal attention to the learning of each and every student. A young worker (paricharak) who stayed and worked in the ashram used to regularly attend his classes and would listen to the Guru's discourses with great attention. He stayed in the ashram, and therefore, happened to listen to the teachings of Sripadaraya being taught to forty different batches! Hence, he sat through forty batches as a student. On the graduation day of the fortieth batch, students from the other thirty-nine batches were invited to attend the ceremony.

The students who attended the graduation ceremony took notice of the paricharak. They ridiculed him that he had not completed his learning in any of the batches. They commented that he was indeed a junior to all those who had passed out and a senior to all the new students who joined. Sripadaraya heard their comments silently. When all of them assembled in front of the Master, he picked up a certain sloka from the texts and asked each and every student of the outgoing batch to explain it. Since all the students were from the same batch, they all gave the same interpretation that they had heard from their Acharya during the classes. The Acharya nodded with approval and then turned to the paricharak who was also sitting in a corner. He asked the paricharak to explain the meaning of the sloka. All the students were astonished. They thought that the paricharak's ignorance would be exposed. They waited to see him totally crestfallen.

The paricharak rose up from his seat, offered his salutations to his Guru, and in all humility, and to the astonishment of all the

students gathered there, rendered forty different interpretations of the same sloka! Every year, the teacher had interpreted the same sloka in a different and unique way, which only he had heard! The paricharak was the only 'student' who had listened to all the forty unique and rare interpretations by the Guru! Not only had he heard the different interpretations, he had also retained them in his memory!

All the scholarly students hung their heads in shame when they heard his explanations. The Guru, Sripadaraya, was immensely pleased with the devoted paricharak-student and blessed him immensely. He advised all the students who had gathered there never to look down upon anyone and to respect all.

The legacy of the Haridasa tradition was continued by Vyasatirtha after Sripadaraya. Vyasatirtha is the guru of Purandaradasa and Kanakadasa.

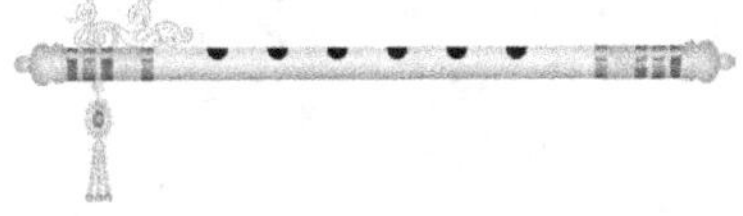

19. How Rama got the Name "Rama Chandra"

The city of Ayodhya was joyously celebrating the birth of Lord Rama - the avatar of Lord Hari. Guru Vasishta gave the divine baby the name - RAMA. He picked up the letter 'Ra' from the 8-lettered 'Om Namo Narayanaya' mantra and 'Ma' from the 5-lettered 'Namah Shivaya' mantra, and combined them to give the most powerful Taraka Mantra: RAMA. Both the letters 'Ra' and 'Ma' are the very LIFE of their corresponding mantras. Without these letters, both the mantras lose their efficacy and the very capacity to bless.

Everyone, including the Gods in the guise of human beings, had come for a glimpse of the child Rama. The devatas, one by one, slowly went up to the cradle to silently offer their prostrations to the Lord without being recognised. When it was the turn of Lord Surya (Lord Sun), he reverentially thanked the Lord for having been born in the Solar dynasty. The All-knowing Lord, in the form of an infant lying in the cradle, smiled and acknowledged him. Next, it was Lord Chandra's (Lord Moon) turn. He went up to the cradle with a very sad face. The Lord asked him what was the matter. Chandra Bhagavan answered that he was upset because he felt that the Lord had neglected and ignored him, and Surya Bhagavan had been given all the importance.

Lord Rama was born in the Solar dynasty in Uttarayan Punyakala (the bright six months of the year), in the bright month of Chaitra (just before summer), in the bright fortnight (Shukla Paksha), during daytime, at noon (abhijit muhurtha) and punarvasu nakshatra—all prominently related to Lord Sun! Of course, Chandra had been sidelined!! The Lord smiled from the cradle and consoled Chandra and told him not to worry. He assured him that in His next avatar, all prominence would be given to Lord Chandra. In His Sri Krishna Avatar, He would be born in the Lunar dynasty, in Dakshinayana Punyakala (the dark six months of the year), in the dark rainy month of Sravana, in the dark fortnight (Krishna Paksha), during midnight, and rohini nakshatra (very dear to Chandra)—all factors prominently related to the Moon. Still, Lord Chandra was not happy. He continued sulking. When the Lord asked him why he was still disappointed, he said he would have to wait for years and years, for Treta Yuga to get over and Dwapara Yuga to start. That was indeed a long...long...wait!

The All-knowing Lord smiled and told him: 'Okay, from today onwards, your name CHANDRA will be added to my name RAMA, and people will address me as RAMACHANDRA. Are you happy now?"

Indeed, Lord Chandra was very happy and satisfied! That is how Lord Sri Rama became Sri RAMACHANDRA!!

Significance: Chandra (Moon) represents our mind. RAMA is the Lord, the very source of life in us. Therefore, RAMA CHANDRA symbolically suggests that we always enshrine the LORD in our MIND.

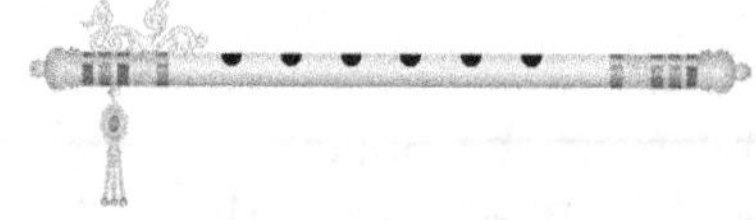

20. Gopis and Their 'Nauka Vihara'

It was a beautiful and pleasant day in Vrindavan. The river Yamuna was flowing gently, the breeze was blowing softly, the cuckoo birds were warbling sweet notes. All the gopis were in their best attire and had assembled on the river bank. They were narrating Krishna's pranks to each other. They decided to embark on a 'Nauka Vihara' - a pleasure-trip in a boat on the Yamuna. Just as they were about to leave, Krishna appeared in front of them and said that he too wished to accompany them on the boat-ride. However, the gopis, who had decided that it was going to be an exclusive trip all for themselves, and by themselves refused to take him along with them. In their vanity, they thought they could manage everything all by themselves, including rowing and steering the boat. Krishna knowingly smiled at their arrogance. He told them that it was not safe to venture into the river all by themselves and he should be allowed to accompany them. They teased him saying that he was only a child after all, and he had no knowledge of rowing and managing the boat; but when he insisted on going with them, they agreed to take him.

All of them got into the boat. They began to feel very important because they were the ones rowing the boat. They sang and danced along with Krishna. He acknowledged each one of them and made them feel very special. The gopis started becoming egoistic and arrogant. Not only did they consider themselves the most beautiful, but also thought themselves extremely privileged to have earned Krishna's complete attention. Above all, He was obliged to them for the boat-ride! They thought nobody could be compared to them. The Lord knowingly smiled and within a fraction of a second, He created a storm. The boat got caught in the storm and it tossed up and down dangerously. The gopis were extremely terrified. The boat was damaged and water started to fill into the boat through holes created by the storm.

Then, they all surrendered and pleaded with Krishna to save them. He said there was only one way out and that was to plug the holes of the boat with their dupattas. They were reluctant to forgo their beautiful attire, but with no other alternative left, they decided to listen to Krishna. With faith in Him, they tried to block the holes of the boat with their dupattas. They were totally and visibly shaken up. They looked absolutely helpless and tearfully surrendered to the Lord, leaving aside all their ego and vanity. The moment they unconditionally surrendered unto the Lord, the storm miraculously subsided and they found themselves safe on the banks of the Yamuna. For the gopis, the 'Nauka Vihara' was a lesson in unquestionable faith, total surrender, and unconditional devotion.

This beautiful incident is called 'Nauka Charitam' - a musical opera (music drama) composed in various ragas by the great Musician-Saint Sri Tyagaraja.

21. Boon to Sleep : Kumbhakarna

Kumbhakarna was Ravana's younger brother, and Vibhishana's elder brother. He was born huge and had a great appetite. He grew up to be a gigantic, powerful and strong Asura, but was also very wise, of good character and a great warrior. Due to all these unique qualities, Indra and the other devatas in Devaloka were worried that Kumbhakarna would be the undisputed winner if he waged a war against Indra.

All the three brothers wanted to acquire boons from Lord Brahma and become powerful. Hence, they meditated on Lord Brahma for many years. Pleased with their penance, Lord Brahma appeared in front of them and asked them what they wished for. Indra was terrified at the very thought of Kumbhakarna asking for boons. He

knew that Kumbhakarna would be unconquerable if he received powers from the Lord. He prayed to Goddess Saraswati who was not only the giver of knowledge but also the bestower of speech. Indra prayed to Saraswati to manipulate Kumbhakarna's speech when he asks for a boon from Lord Brahma.

Kumbhakarna wanted to ask for Indrasana (Indra's throne) but ended up asking for Nidrasana (state of sleep), and instead of asking for Nirdevatvam (non-existence of Devatas), he asked for Nidraavatvam (continuous sleep)! The boon was granted. Kumbhakarna quickly realized his mistake and requested Lord Brahma to undo the boon. But, once granted, the boon could not be reversed. Hence, Kumbhakarna would continuously sleep for six months. When he would wake up, he would eat to his full for a day and go back to sleep again for the next six months.

During the fierce battle between Lord Rama and Ravana, Ravana's army suffered great losses. At that time, Ravana decided to wake up Kumbhakarna. It is said that a thousand elephants were required to wake him up. When Kumbhakarna realized that Ravana had captured Rama's wife, Sita, he tried to convince Ravana to return Sita to Rama. But Ravana was stubborn and refused. Finally, Kumbhakarna went to the battlefield. After a fierce battle between Rama and him, Kumbakarna was finally killed by Lord Rama.

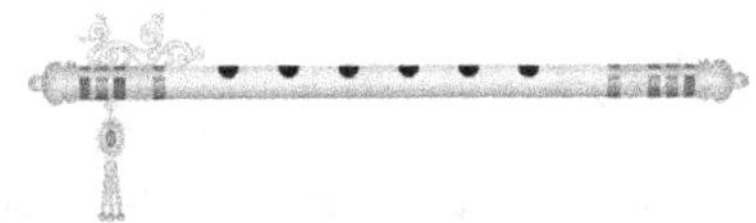

22. The Story of Andal

Vishnuchittar, also known as Periyazhwar (9th Century), was the first among the twelve prominent Vaishnava saints of Tamil Nadu born in Srivilliputhur near Madurai. He was a great devotee of Lord Vishnu and has contributed to the philosophical and theological ideas of Vaishnavism. His major contributions include Thirupallandu and Periya Azhwar Thirumozhi.

Vishnuchittar was childless and this worried him. He prayed to God to bless him with a child. One day, when he was walking in his garden, he found a baby girl lying near a Tulasi plant. It is said that Mother Earth (Bhoomi Devi) herself had appeared as a child in answer to his prayers. He took the child home, named her Kothai, and brought her up as his daughter. He would teach her songs and tell her stories about Lord Vishnu and His glories.

Hence, the little girl grew up in a divine atmosphere of Bhakti. As she grew up, her devotion and love for Sri Hari also grew to such an extent that she decided she would only get married to the Lord. As the days progressed, her resolve to marry the Lord only strengthened.

Vishnuchittar used to make beautiful flower garlands, take them to the temple, and offer them to Lord Ranganatha daily. This was his devoted nitya seva to the Lord. Kothai, who considered herself the bride-to-be of the Lord, used to take the garland, wear it, and admire herself in the mirror. She would then remove the garland and place it in the basket to be taken to the temple. Vishnuchittar was unaware of this and used to take the same used garland and offer it to the Lord. Hence, for days, the garland worn by Kodhai was being offered to the Lord.

One day, Vishnuchittar saw his daughter wearing the garland made for the Lord. He was shocked. How could anyone wear what was meant for the Lord? He was extremely upset and scolded her. He told her never to repeat the act again. On that day, there was no garland for the Lord. That night, the Lord came in Periyazhwar's dream and told him that he liked the garlands worn by Kothai and henceforth, He would only accept garlands worn by her. From then onwards, Kodhai came to be known as 'Andal' - one who ruled over the Lord.

Andal's yearning for the Lord increased day by day and her devotional outpourings are called Thiruppavai and

Nacchiaar Thirumozhi. When Vishnuchittar was searching for a suitable groom for Andal, she expressed her keen desire to get married to the Lord. He told her that there are 108 Divya Kshetras of Lord Vishnu. She asked him to narrate the glory of the Deity of each Kshetra. She was thrilled to hear about the Lord of Mathura, smiled when she heard about the Lord of Tirumala, happy to hear about the Lord of the Azhagar Temple (Madurai), but was ecstatic when she heard about the Lord of Srirangam! She chose Lord Sri Ranganatha of Srirangam as her husband.

Her father was worried about how he ought to proceed. The same night, the Lord appeared in his dream and asked him to bring Andal to the temple. Simultaneously, the Lord appeared in the temple priest's dream and instructed him to accompany Vishnuchittar's daughter from Srivilliputhur to Srirangam. The Lord also told the Pandyan King, Vallabhadevan, to make arrangements for the wedding. Accordingly, Andal, in bridal attire, was taken to Srirangam in a pearl palanquin. She reached the temple of Srirangam. In the presence of everyone assembled there, she walked into the sanctum sanctorum of Lord Ranganatha and merged with Him.

Bhoomi Devi, who had come to Vishnuchittar in the form of Andal, is worshiped in Srivilliputhur. Even to this day for Tirupati Brahmotsavam, garlands worn by Andal in Srivilliputhur temple are sent to the Lord Venkateshwara Temple in Tirupati. These traditional garlands are made of tulasi, sevanthi and sampangi flowers. These garlands are worn by Lord Venkateshwara during the Garuda seva procession.

23. Lord Hanuman's Guru

Surya Bhagavan stands for the Light of Knowledge and Wisdom. He is the All-knowing Silent Witness of the whole world. He represents the World Teacher, the Giver of both subjective and objective knowledge. It is said that the Vedas are under the care of Surya Bhagavan. Young Hanuman wanted to have Lord Surya alone as his Guru. One day in the morning, Hanuman took a big leap and reached Surya Bhagavan. With folded hands he approached Lord Surya, and requested him to accept him as his disciple.

Surya Bhagavan was very pleased with Hanuman's request. However, since he is constantly on the move, he told Hanuman that he could not stop at any point of time to teach him. Hanuman came up with a solution. He told Lord Surya that he could continue

his celestial journey without a break and still teach him. Hanuman told Surya Bhagavan to continue moving forward and teach him, while he would face his Guru and keep moving backwards at the same speed!

Surya Bhagavan was very pleased at the student's loving persistence and agreed. In this way, Hanuman quickly grasped all that was taught to him by Lord Surya. He studied the four books of Knowledge (Vedas), the six systems of philosophies (Darshanas), the sixty-four Arts (Kalas) and mastered the nine Vyakaranas (Grammar) along with the one hundred and eight mysteries of Tantra. After he completed his education, it was time for him to offer guru dakshina to his Guru. Hanuman asked his Guru what he could offer him, but Lord Surya said that he was more than happy to have a sishya like Hanuman, and he did not want anything from his disciple. However, Hanuman insisted. So, Surya Bhagavan asked Hanuman to look after the welfare of his son, Sugriva (the prince of Kishkinda), and help him later in life. Hanuman agreed.

Hanuman kept his promise and always stood by Sugriva. He also helped him get acquainted with Lord Rama. When Sugriva became the King of Kishkinda, Hanuman was his most trusted minister.

The famous 'Surya Namaskar' is generally attributed to Hanuman, an outcome of his utter reverence and gratitude to his Guru, Surya Bhagavan.

24. Ganesha's Insatiable Hunger!

Kubera was the treasurer of the heavens and was very proud of his immense wealth. He was a miser too! In order to show off his wealth and richness, he decided to organize a grand event. He invited all the devatas to his golden palace.

All the gods who visited Kubera's palace had a sumptuous meal and glorified Kubera and his hospitality. However, he was not satisfied. He wanted Lord Shiva to visit him as well, and appreciate his wealth and riches.

With this in mind, Kubera visited Kailash and requested Lord Shiva to accept his invitation for a meal. Lord Shiva was aware of Kubera's pride and his extreme attachment to his wealth. He decided to teach Kubera a lesson. He accepted the invitation, but said that all his attendants would accompany him. That was a huge number to feed! Kubera pleaded with the Lord, saying that he wanted the Lord alone so that he could attend to him exclusively. The Lord refused saying that if he came, his attendants would

also accompany him. Kubera was disappointed. Seeing Kubera's crestfallen face, Lord Shiva said that instead of all of them he was willing to send his son, Ganesha, as a substitute. Immediately, Kubera became happy! Only one person to feed and that too a child! He couldn't bargain for more than this! As Kubera was about to leave, accompanied by Ganesha, the Lord warned Kubera that Ganesha was a voracious eater. Kubera confidently told Shiva that he could handle Ganesha's appetite.

When they reached the palace, Kubera took Ganesha around so that he could see the beauty and grandeur of his palace. However, Ganesha told Kubera that he was very hungry. Ganesha went straight to the dining place and sat down to eat his food. Kubera immediately ordered his attendants to bring food. The food was brought in a beautiful golden plate, with a variety of dishes and sweets. No sooner had the food been placed before him, Ganesha ate everything up within a fraction of a second. More food was brought and served, but it immediately disappeared into Ganesha's mouth again.

It is customary to feed a person till they say that they've had their fill. Hence, Kubera kept on ordering for more food to be brought out. The food kept on coming from inside, Ganesha kept on consuming it, until the kitchen was totally empty. Kubera told Ganesha that not even a morsel of food was left in the palace. Ganesha got angry that Kubera could not feed him and satisfy his hunger as he had promised. He started consuming whatever he could lay his hands on. The golden utensils, the beautiful furniture, and even the pillars of the palace about which Kubera had boasted; everything disappeared into Ganesha's

mouth. Kubera pleaded with him to stop, but Ganesha continued demanding more food. He even threatened to eat Kubera himself.

Kubera was terrified. He realized his mistake and ran to Kailash with Ganesha following close behind. When they reached Kailash, Kubera humbly fell at Lord Shiva's feet. He begged the Lord to forgive him for his arrogance and save him from Ganesha's anger. The Lord turned to Ganesha and lovingly gave him a handful of roasted rice flakes to eat. Immediately, Ganesha's hunger was satisfied.

The Lord advised Kubera that wealth had its place in the scheme of things, but wealth alone cannot fulfil all our needs.

Wealth is not to be hoarded, but should be used and shared intelligently. Only then Wealth is a blessing!

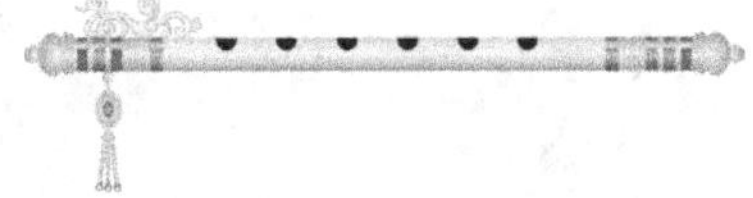

25. Sri Vidya Upasaka: Dikshitar

Muthuswami Dikshitar (1775 - 1835) was one of the greatest Musician-Saints of his time. He is one among the Carnatic Music Trinity, along with Saint Thyagaraja and Shyama Sastri.

Dikshitar's father was Ramaswami Dikshitar. He was a Sanskrit scholar and an accomplished musician who lived in Tiruvarur, in Tamil Nadu. When Dikshitar turned twenty-five, the great Chidambaranatha Yogi of Varanasi visited their house. He requested Ramaswami to send Dikshitar with him for further education. His father agreed and Dikshitar went to Varanasi. He was initiated into 'Sri Vidya Upasana'. His Guru told him

to constantly worship Sri Annapurneswari, the bestower of material needs (Bhukti), as well as liberation (Mukti). He mastered the scriptures, the science of mantras, astrology,   and music. He was also an expert in playing the veena. He was influenced by Hindustani classical music and Western band music.

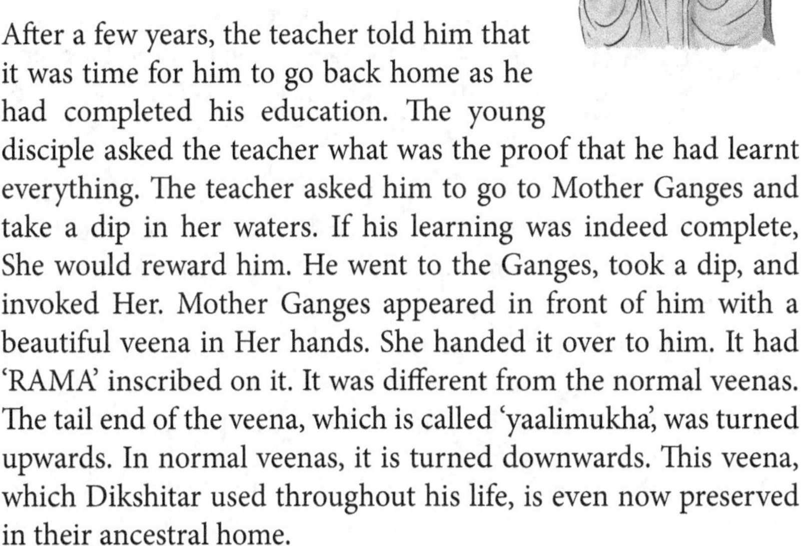

After a few years, the teacher told him that it was time for him to go back home as he had completed his education. The young disciple asked the teacher what was the proof that he had learnt everything. The teacher asked him to go to Mother Ganges and take a dip in her waters. If his learning was indeed complete, She would reward him. He went to the Ganges, took a dip, and invoked Her. Mother Ganges appeared in front of him with a beautiful veena in Her hands. She handed it over to him. It had 'RAMA' inscribed on it. It was different from the normal veenas. The tail end of the veena, which is called 'yaalimukha', was turned upwards. In normal veenas, it is turned downwards. This veena, which Dikshitar used throughout his life, is even now preserved in their ancestral home.

With the blessings of his teacher, and with this unique veena gifted to him by the Mother of Knowledge, Dikshitar travelled back. He arrived at Tiruttani, one of the six famous abodes of Kartikeya in Tamil Nadu. Dikshitar was sitting and meditating on the Lord on the steps of the temple, when Lord Kartikeya came in the disguise of an elderly man, asked him to open his mouth, and put sugar candy into his mouth. Immediately, he disappeared. At that very moment, he composed a beautiful kriti on Kartikeya with the mudra (signature) GURU-GUHA. Kartikeya also known as GUHA had come to him as his GURU.

Dikshitar has composed songs on almost all deities, all pilgrimage centres, and brought into the kritis the uniqueness and speciality of them all. Along with Sangeeta sastra, he incorporated the 'mantra sastra' into his songs. Therefore, if someone is able to render them with correct pronunciation and bhava, with a little understanding of its meaning, it will bring prosperity to the singer as well as the listener - singing of his keerthans is equivalent to chanting the mantras.

There are many instances of Dikshitar bringing relief and solace to individuals, as well as the community, through his keerthans. With a Kriti in raga Amruthavarshini, he brought the rains down on the parched land of Ettayyapuram (Tamil Nadu). He also brought health back to his disciple, Tambiyappan, by warding off the evil effects (graha dosha) of Jupiter, by composing a kriti on that planet.

On the eve of Deepavali in 1835, after he had finished Devi Puja, he had a vision of Sri Annapurneswari and sang 'Ehi Annapurne' - his last kriti. He remembered what his Guru had told him and knew it was time for him to leave his body. He asked his disciples who had gathered there to sing his composition 'Meenakshi me mudam dehi' (Meenakshi, bestow your grace upon me) in the Raga Gamakakriya. When they sang the lines: 'Meena lochani pasha mochani' (O! Fish-eyed One, who cuts asunder the knots of bondage), he asked them to repeat the phrases once more. As they were repeating them, Dikshitar uttered, "Shive pahi, Shive pahi, Shive pahi," and left his physical body. He merged eternally with the Mother of the Universe whom he had invoked and worshipped all his life.

His compositions called 'Kamalamba Nava-avarana Krithis', which are full of mystic significance, are rendered even today with great religious fervour during the Navaratri festival.

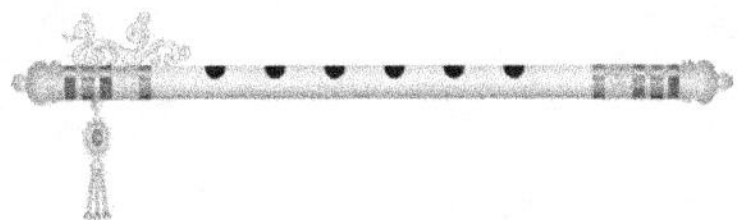

www.ingramcontent.com/pod-product-compliance
Lightning Source LLC
Chambersburg PA
CBHW061259140726
47998CB00006B/2284